Made in the USA
Monee, IL
18 May 2022

96644804R00069